AΩ

Alpha to Omega

Amy Adams Squire

*Desha & Rick —
Hope Jesus can
still find you.
Ha!
Amy*

Rocking Horse Publishing, St. Louis, Missouri

First printing, September, 2016

Copyright © Amy Adams Squire, 2016
All rights reserved.

ISBN 10: 0-9979894-1-6
ISBN 13: 978-0-9979894-1-0

Cover design by Shannon Yarbrough, St. Louis, Missouri
Cover art by Amy Adams Squire
All illustrations original art by Amy Adams Squire

Many of the characters and events in this book are fictitious. Many are not. It is hereby left to the reader to make that determination.

www.RockingHorsePublishing.com

DEDICATION

To my mom Laura Squire, who taught me to read with a critical eye, to think with an open mind, to live for someone besides myself, and to love without regret.

The Bible is a curious compilation of mythology, mystery, history, poetry, advice, and political commentary. I am no theologian and have but the most basic training in literary criticism. It doesn't take a scholar, however, to understand that the Biblical canon that we now use is heavily edited and translated. In recent times, various people have even had the audacity to put their own names on the Holy Bible, from King James to Eugene Peterson.

The Bible has been a great source for big-screen entertainment, capitalized on by Hollywood directors such as Cecil B. DeMille, Mel Gibson, and Darren Aronofsy. It is perfectly amenable to high drama, exotic scenery, and casts of thousands.

It is the casts of thousands which are the focus of this work. I have taken but a small sampling of characters from the Hebrew and Christian canons to illustrate the absurdity and resiliency of human relationships as they pertain to one another and to the Divine.

I look at the stories of God's intervention in human affairs from a very modern perspective. You will find modern cultural references and idioms throughout. These stories are highly imaginative, and I suggest that if playing fast and loose with Scripture is likely to make you uneasy, you proceed with caution. It is my hope that despite the unrepentant cynicism contained herein, you will be able to extract some nugget of truth and hope from each story. Enjoy.

Finally, a big shout out to Robin Tidwell for taking a chance, Rev. Cynthia Espeseth for taking an interest, and my father the late Gray Squire, who thought everything I accomplished was wonderful.

Amy Adams Squire
Seattle, 2016

CONTENTS

PART I: ONCE UPON A TIME

1. Before the Beginning
2. In-A-Gadda-Da-Vida
3. Eviction Notice
4. Sibling Rivalry
5. Back to the Drawing Board
6. Say What?
7. Road Trip to Destiny
8. World Wrestling Entertainment
9. The Dreamer
10. The Burning Bush
11. To Don't List
12. Babylonian Idol
13. We Are Family
14. Beauty and the Beast
15. Bel and El
16. Errand Boy

PART II: TURN THE PAGE

17. Unplanned Parenthood
18. Born in a Barn
19. Shall We Gather at the River?
20. You Have No Power Here!
21. Jesus Turns Pro
22. Attitudes
23. The Full Meal Deal
24. Advanced Life-Saving
25. Good as New

PART III: BRING IT ON HOME

26. Fire in the Hole
27. Saul's Excellent Adventure
28. Grand Finale

AΩ

CHAPTER 1

BEFORE THE BEGINNING
(From Genesis 1 and 2)

Once upon a time (before there was time), in a galaxy far, far away, lived an ineffable, omniscient, omnipotent being. This being was pure thought, without conception and without expiration. For the sake of convenience and consistency, we will refer to this being as God.

God had created many universes and dimensions, each more wondrous than the one before it. God had many helpers in these artistic endeavors. God created angels, spirits, deities, demigods, demiurges, sprites, nymphs, elves, and muses, to name a few. Each presented an aspect of God. Most were given to acts of whimsy and flights of fancy. On any given day, you could find them chasing each other around the planets, tossing lightning bolts like darts, and blowing kisses, which often turned into giant windstorms.

Itching to apply for a new patent, God decided to create a new species, which would occupy a universe and classification just beneath the angels. So God gathered the celestial helpers in the conference room and said, "Let us make a new species called 'Human' in our image, according to our likeness."

This endeavor would require some planning. After a break for coffee and donuts, the participating artists, scientists, and engineers divided up into focus groups to hammer out the details.

1

CHAPTER 2

IN-A-GADDA-DA-VIDA*
(From Genesis 1 and 2)

It was unanimously agreed upon that before the specifications for the new creature could be finalized, a magnificent home should first be realized. It would be a home that supplied everything the new model would need to flourish. It was further concluded that this dwelling should be a garden.

Now the planet of Gaia, called Earth, had been placed in the heavens millions of years before, and now it was ready to accommodate life. A garden had been planted in the East. It was called Gan Eden, meaning "the Garden of God." A great river flowed out of Eden. And the river divided into four branches. The first is Pishon, which sounds like something you might find under the hood of your car. The second is Gishon. The third is Tigris, and the fourth is Euphrates.

These watered the land, which was filled with all manner of botanicals: herbs, vegetables, fruits, flowers, grasses, trees, healing plants, and, of course, cannabis, which turned out to be a particular favorite of the new species.

When all was ready, God took the plans and went to his studio. He took a bucket of mud and slapped it on the potter's

2

AΩ

wheel. He fashioned the clay mud into a two-legged being that was beautifully symmetrical. Then God took the finished product to the Garden and blew into its mouth the breath of life. Seeing that the new creature was the only one of its kind, God thought that a companion might be welcome. This is where art and science meet.

God went to the lab and put the newly minted creature into a suspended animation. Then God extracted some DNA. From the DNA, God grew a companion, alike yet different. It seemed fitting that each should have a distinct identity. So God called the first one Adam, which means "the first human." The second, God called Eve, which means "the Mother of All Living." And thus was born a new race with free will, intelligence, and, of course, opposable thumbs.

---

*This title is actually the title of a 1968 song by Iron Butterfly. It means "In the Garden of Eden."

CHAPTER 3

EVICTION NOTICE
(From Genesis 3)

I neglected to mention earlier that the lush Garden of Eden was filled with not only every conceivable plant, but also with a diverse assemblage of animal life, from one-celled amoebas, blissfully self-dividing, to exceedingly complex primates such as the chimpanzee, a first cousin to the human, although not nearly as attractive.

Among the myriad taxonomic classifications were the reptiles, an aloof bunch. One suborder, which, although low in rank among the Animal Kingdom, proved to be most vexing, was indeed was the very undoing of the lofty two-legged human. This cunning creature was called the serpent.

Now in the center of Eden, God had planted a giant tree. This magnificent arbor grew tall and stately, rising above all the other trees. Its rings numbered in the thousands, and its leaves were as large as dinosaur feet. God called this The Tree of the Knowledge of Good and Evil. (Personally, I hold God responsible for introducing this seemingly innocuous duality into the perfect unity which was the Garden. However, that is fodder for a philosophical debate on another occasion.)

ΑΩ

Supposing Eve to be the more malleable of the two humans, the serpent found her playing croquet one day and said, "So, Eve. How's it going?"

"Very well, thank you," she replied.

"Don't you ever get bored?" asked the serpent.

"What is bored?" asked Eve.

"Um. You know, wishing you had ssssomething more entertaining and challenging to do."

"I hadn't really thought about it," said Eve, giving the red ball a solid smack with her mallet.

"Ever thought of having a midnight ssssnack from the big tree in the middle there?"

"God said that we may not eat of its fruit or even touch the tree. If we do, we shall surely die."

"God likes to exaggerate," said the serpent. "You won't die. Your third eye will be opened, and you will gain knowledge of good and evil, and become like God."

Eve was very fond of God and thought that being like God would be very nice indeed. So Eve went to the great tree and plucked a large piece of luscious yellow fruit from it (somebody made up that stuff about the apple; perhaps it made for a better Baroque painting). She took a large bite of the succulent treat. When she had finished, she decided to share some of the fruit with Adam.

Knowing that his plan was successful, the serpent withdrew.

Eve found Adam having a nap in the hammock. "Adam, wake up. I have a gift for you."

Eve showed Adam the fruit and told him what the serpent had said about becoming wise. "You know, dear, you're not the brightest candle in the menorah," she said. "Together we can be wise and talk with God as equals."

So Adam ate the fruit, and the two became very smart and introspective. This knowledge, though wonderful, was new and frightening. So they went together and hid in a cave. In the shank of the evening, God came to the Garden and called Adam and Eve to come sit a spell in the Adirondack chairs he had carefully arranged. As soon as they emerged from the cave, God knew what they had done.

"What is the number of pi?" God asked.

"It is 3.14, give or take," said Adam.

"You two have been at the fruit of the forbidden tree haven't you?" asked God.

Adam deflected, "Eve gave me the fruit."

Eve became defensive. "The serpent told me I would become wise like you, God."

God clapped his hand to his forehead, "The serpent!" he exclaimed. "I should have known. I'll deal with him later. As for you two: you break my heart. I gave you everything, and you couldn't do the only thing I asked of you."

Adam looked at the ground and dug his big toe in the dirt, thinking, "Uh-oh. Dad's mad."

God, in a rage, shouted, "You have until dawn to get your stuff packed. The Garden will be forever lost to you. You will leave Eden and make your own way on the earth. You will become slaves of your own desires, grow old, and die."

Adam and Eve were very sad. They did as God commanded and went quietly away, clinging to each other. And God posted an angel with a sword of flame at the entrance to Eden so that no human might ever enter it again.

God returned to his home among the stars and wept bitterly, for he had failed his creation.

AΩ

CHAPTER 4

SIBLING RIVALRY
(From Genesis 4)

Adam and Eve, having fallen from grace, as it were, were no longer able to reproduce asexually. This is not to suggest that sexual reproduction is a bad thing. Far from it. It can be quite fun and entertaining. It's just more difficult and infinitely more random. You never know if that EPT stick is going to show + or -.

So the two renegades knocked boots a couple of times, and Eve bore two lovely sons, Cain and Abel.

After a difficult puberty, Cain became a farmer. Abel was a largely untroubled youth who got good grades and became a shepherd.

Apparently knowledge comes at a price. In this case, Eve and her trusty sidekick Adam could no longer walk with God in the Garden. And life outside the perimeter was mean and hard. Still, the couple remembered and honored their Creator and taught their offspring to do likewise.

When the time came to return to God an offering of the first and the best of their winnings, Cain brought the Lord some of his harvest. He put the sheaves of corn and wheat in a large

7

wicker basket and accented it with fruits and flowers. Then he put a large red ribbon around the basket and placed it at the altar. It was a fine looking gift, and Cain was sure that God would be pleased.

For his offering, Abel slaughtered a couple of unblemished lambs (remember that this was in the days long before PETA). He laid the exsanguinated beasts on the altar fire. God was quite partial to the mutton BBQ but turned up his nose at the lovely gift basket. The rejection pissed off Cain royally.

God said to Cain, "Do you not know that an acceptable offering comes from a heart filled with pure intentions?"

Rather than bother to examine his conscience to see what might have made his offering unacceptable, Cain threw a hissy fit and kicked the basket over. Then he stormed off to find his brother. Jealously grew quickly in Cain's heart, and when he found his brother, he lobbed one mighty right cross at Abel's head, killing him instantly.

Cain felt vindicated, but by his action doomed his descendants to a lust for blood.

ΑΩ

CHAPTER 5

BACK TO THE DRAWING BOARD
(From Genesis 6 and 7)

THE WINGED ONES

By the time Noah came along in the span of human evolution, the whole of creation was completely out of control. It was a proper shambles by anyone's standards. History predictably points the finger at humankind for this melee, but they had heavenly help. The winged ones, or Nephilim (sons of God), who were supposed to be watching out for the two-leggeds, went AWOL from heaven.

Thanks to Eve, the Mother of All Living, human women were smart, talented, and comely. The winged ones fell in lust with the daughters of men. (Maybe a life of celestial celibacy makes you horny. Who knows?) So the sons of God took the daughters of men as their significant others. Their offspring, being the product of two different species, were hideous, humongous, dull-witted, and violent. These first-generation behemoths wreaked havoc wherever they went, thrashing about, eating everything that wasn't nailed down, and fornicating with anything that couldn't get away.

The corruption perpetrated by the winged ones spread across the earth until all of humankind looked like a global Ted Nugent concert: vulgar, capricious, aggressive, sexually inappropriate, selfish, and immature.

So God, seeing that he had lost his command, decided to scrap the whole misbegotten project. Pacing around his laboratory, God sighed and began to erase the blackboard, saying, "I will blot out from the face of the earth all creation—people together with animals and creeping things and birds of the air, for I am sorry that I have made them."

ENTER NOAH

If there was one thing for which God had a particular gift, it would be talent-scouting the most righteous individuals of the age—an attribute which had saved humankind from total annihilation on several occasions.

Just as God was about to make all-gone with humanity, Noah caught his attention. Noah found favor in the sight of the

AΩ

Lord and walked with God, which was a poetic way of saying that Noah was a pious player.

So God explained to Noah, "I have determined to make an end of all flesh. Your kind has become a whiny, contentious lot, pretty irredeemable from what I can see. But you, Noah, make me happy. Therefore, I have chosen you to be the new primogenitor of your species.

"You will construct a freighter to my exact specifications, and you and your family will gather two of every living thing—except the unicorn*—and take them aboard the ark. Then I will cause a great flood to cover the earth. The deluge will last forty days and forty nights."

"Let me stop you right there, Majesty," said Noah, an intensely pragmatic man who had already picked up on several logistical problems. "Have you considered the implications of being shut up for an extended period with a nautical zoo, most likely prone to seasickness? Remember, I'm the one who has to feed and clean up after them."

"You have been faithful to me for many years, Noah," said God. "Now I will demonstrate my faith in you to rise to the challenge."

"Oh, brilliant," thought Noah. "God thinks I can manage being a janitor, doctor, and social worker. Lucky me."

"When the floodwaters recede, I will re-establish my covenant with humankind through you," said God.

"Um . . . thank you, Lord—I think," replied Noah warily.

---

*The unicorn was actually one of God's favorite creations. But the unicorn was a rambunctious creature, careless about stabbing people in the hind end with its long curlicue horn and farting rainbows at inappropriate times. So God thought it might be best to let that one go while the opportunity presented itself.

Amy Adams Squire

AΩ

CHAPTER 6

SAY WHAT?
(From Genesis 11.1-9)

Legend has it that Noah's nautical circus dropped anchor on the summit of the sacred Mount Ararat, located in what is now eastern Turkey. After discharging the cargo (a process that took several months because of pregnant elephants and stubborn mules), Noah set about re-establishing civilization, which he did expertly, his offspring generating many nations.

Miraculously, the whole earth had retained one language in common. It was the pre-Semitic language of Eve and Adam—a combination of concepts transmitted telepathically and spoken words understood by everyone.

As Noah's clan spread out from the East, some of them came to a plain in the land known as Shinar, a region in Mesopotamia. There they settled like a bad chest cold.

Now humankind is a restless, distracted lot, constantly craving entertainment. Bored with rebuilding civilization, the Shinar settlers instead decided to build a monument that would reach into the heavens until it touched the very throne of The Most High. But The Most High was having none of it. Following the cacophony of laborers baking bricks and bellowing oxen

13

dragging the bricks around on planks, God descended from the stars to see what all the fuss was about.

None too pleased with the mess the two-leggeds had made with their giant Legos and fearing that they would succeed in breaching the veil between the worlds, God decided to throw a spanner in the works. God remembered that he had taken an oath not to destroy the two-legged race again, so he cleverly confounded their tongues so that each tribe spoke a different language. And we all know what a shit storm it is when communications are down.

As God had hoped, the humans abandoned their grand architectural project and gathered into clans according to language. They left Shinar and spread out with all haste to parts unknown, perplexed, confused, and annoyed that no one could understand them.

What did you say? *Was hast du gesagt? Kion vi diris? Qu'est-ce que vous avez dit? ¿Qué dijiste? O que você disse? Что ты сказал? He aha la oe i olelo mai ai? Quid dicam vobis? Τι είπες? Mwati chiyani? Vad sa du? Ulisema nini?* आपने क्या कहा?

ΑΩ

CHAPTER 7

ROAD TRIP TO DESTINY
(From Genesis 12-17)

It seems the Lord was always bossing the ancients around. Live here. Leave there. Do this, but don't do that. Failure to comply could result in a smiting.

So God spoke to Abram and said, "Pack the Winnebago. You're going on a road trip. Leave your father Terah's home in Haran, and travel to the land that I will show you. It's a surprise." Abram was justifiably wary of the Almighty's "surprises."

"Not only will I guide you to a new land, but also I will make you the progenitor of a great nation."

"Well, you're just full of surprises, aren't you?" said Abram, stuffing his socks into a duffle bag.

Thus, Abram packed up all his worldly possessions and set off with his wife Sarai, his nephew Lot, and various neighbors and relations.

No road trip would be complete without the occasional mishap: a flat tire, a pregnant camel, car sickness, accidentally leaving the baby in the motel, etc., and this adventure was no different. First came the famine, which took Abram and Sarai to Egypt in search of food. Then Abram and Lot went their

15

separate ways because their combined possessions were so great that they could not live together. Crazy, huh? Abram settled in Canaan, and Lot went to Sodom. There Lot was taken into captivity by a wicked king, of which there was no short supply in those days. In fact, you could pretty much have your pick of greedy, evil potentates.

Upon hearing of Lot's predicament, Abram led exactly 318 men on a successful rescue mission. To honor Abram's efforts, King Melchizedek (say that 3 times fast) of Salem blessed Abram. This was apparently quite a big deal.

PHASE I

At last, the word of the Lord came to Abram by way of a cinematic vision. "Do not be afraid, Abram. I am your shield. Your reward shall be very great."

Abram replied, "O Lord God, what can you possibly give me that would be more valuable than an heir? For I continue to be childless, and the heir of my house is Eliezer of Damascus."

It would have made things much simpler if Abram could have bequeathed his vast estate to his wife Sarai. But no, in those days, women were worth about as much as a couple of goats and a tent. So probate had to go the long way 'round.

But God said, "No. Eliezer will not be your heir. Your very own son will inherit your portion."

God led Abram out into the night and told him to gaze at the vast numbers of stars in the sky and said, "As the infinite numbers of the stars in the heavens, so shall the number of your descendants be."

"Sweet!" exclaimed Abram, and he believed God, and it was reckoned to him as righteousness.

AΩ

Now, when Abram was 86, he fathered a son by a slave, and the boy was named Ishmael. Ishmael was to be the father of a great desert people. Phase I completed.

PHASE II

When Abram was 99 years old, God promised him another son by his wife Sarai. He was to be born the following year and would be called Isaac.

So God, who had a penchant for making covenants with people, made one with Abram. "You shall be the ancestor of a multitude of nations. No longer shall your name be Abram. Your name shall now be Abraham. This is my covenant, which you shall keep, between me and you and your offspring after you: You shall circumcise the flesh of your foreskins, and it shall be a sign of the covenant between me and you."

Okay. Just so we're clear. God made a contract with a guy by adding two letters to his name and surgically altering his penis. That certainly left women out of the covenant.

The only reason I can think of for using the male member to make a covenant was simply to commemorate the fact that at the advanced age of 99, Abraham could still get it up long enough to get his wife pregnant without the aid of Viagra.

CHAPTER 8

WORLD WRESTLING ENTERTAINMENT
(From Genesis 32)

Jacob and Esau came along later in the Biblical saga. Like their ancestors Cain and Abel, brothers have a way of falling out with each other. As our story opens, Jacob had spent the day devising a scheme to reunite with his brother Esau. No small feat that. In those days, long before public Facebook humiliations and confessions, courtesy, protocol, and appeasement were matters of life and death and involved complicated rituals.

Having devised a way to reconnect with his estranged elder brother, Jacob sent his two wives (lucky guy) and eleven children across the Ford of Jabbock. This left Jacob on his own, and with such a prolific family, this actually might have been a welcome break.

As is often the case in Biblical narrative, sometimes characters just appear and disappear without warning and for no apparent reason. This was the case with Jacob. A strange man apparently leaped out from behind a rock and challenged Jacob to a sort of old-school wrestling match.

AΩ

They struggled all day (without the nervous-system-enhancing benefits of Red Bull, I might add). When it was clear that Jacob could not be pinned, the mysterious stranger gave Jacob a whack on the pelvis, completely dislocating the hip joint.

If you have ever had a hip replacement, then you are thoroughly familiar with the excruciating sensation of bone on bone. But even this agony was not enough to stop our hero Jacob.

The stranger finally surrendered and implored Jacob to release him.

"Not until you bless me," said Jacob, a rather curious request given the circumstances. Can you imagine Dean Ambrose asking Triple H* to bless him before leaving the ring?

So the man said to Jacob, "I don't do generic blessings. What is your name?"

"Jacob."

"The blessing I give you is that of a new name. Henceforth, you shall be called 'Israel,' for you have striven with both God and man and have, rather amazingly, prevailed."

The stranger departed, and Israel named the site of the exchange Peniel, because he had seen God face to face and lived to tell the tale, a pronounced limp notwithstanding.

---

*Dean Ambrose and Triple H are professional wrestlers in the WWE.

Amy Adams Squire

AΩ

CHAPTER 9

THE DREAMER
(From Genesis 37)

Israel—the patriarch formerly known as Jacob—became the Father of the Israelites. This was not just an honorary title, like OBE*. It was a fitting designation. With the very kind assistance of several presumably willing women, Israel managed to produce twelve sons who would become the leaders of the twelve tribes of Israel: Reuben, Simeon, Levi, Judah, Dan, Naphtali, Gad, Asher, Issachar, Zebulun, Joseph, and Benjamin. He also had a daughter named Dinah in case anyone is interested.

Although Benjamin was technically the youngest, Joseph was Israel's favorite because he was a blessing conceived late in Israel's AARP years. As a token of his affection for Joseph, Israel had a spectacular multi-colored tunic woven for him. (Christian Lacroix had nothing on this design.) None of Israel's other sons ever received such a gift.

Although they should probably have been annoyed with their father for his overt favoritism, they resented Joseph instead, demonstrating once again that fraternity is fraught with

21

obstacles. But Joseph was an open-hearted free-spirit who forgave and ignored his brothers' petty jealousies.

Israel and his burgeoning family lived in Canaan, and sheep herding was the bulk of the family business. (Desert life was somewhat limiting in terms of career options.) By the age of seventeen, Joseph was working as an assistant to the brothers by Israel's wives, Bilhah and Zilpah. Joseph reported to his father that the brothers goofed off a lot. They drank wine, smoked, and gambled, leaving the sheep to fend for themselves. If you've ever met a sheep, you will have observed that sheep are hapless creatures who require regular assistance with decision-making and should not be left to their own devices for extended periods.

Joseph's dutiful accounts really irked the brothers. Showing a great lack of maturity, Gad called Joseph a tattletale, and the brothers ostracized Joseph from their activities and conversations. Oblivious to the brothers ill will, one day Joseph unwisely shared an unflattering dream with them as they watched the sheep bleat and shuffle.

"Listen to this dream I had, guys!"

Reuben, many years older than Joseph, looked at the lad with disdain, but Joseph continued, impervious to Reuben's obvious contempt.

"I dreamed that the sun, the moon, and eleven stars were all bowing down to me."

Later Joseph recounted this same dream to his father who, along with Joseph's siblings, felt a bit miffed and confused. "Are your mother and I and all your brothers besides supposed to bow before you?"

Reuben encapsulated his feelings in a less tactful response: "Get lost, you arrogant little butt wipe."

And so the brothers began to plot their revenge on Joseph.

One day, when Israel had sent Joseph to find and report back on his brothers, they lay in wait for him, planning to kill

AΩ

him. Although Reuben was by far the most vocal in his disdain for Joseph and his dreams, he drew the line when it came to fratricide. "Let's just throw him down the empty well," proposed Reuben, hoping to teach Joseph a lesson and at some point rescue him to be reunited with their father.

The brothers agreed to spare his life. So when Joseph finally found them, they took his beautiful robe, gave him a thrashing, and tossed him into the well. "There you go, Dreamer Boy. Dream your way out of this!"

The brothers sat down to eat. As they prepared and consumed their repast, they concocted a tale to explain Joseph's disappearance to their father. Talk about dreamers! Each account they came up with was more fantastic than the next.

"We could say that he was taken up into heaven by a great UFO," said Asher.

"Or we could say that he ran away to join the circus," Levi suggested.

"No. No. No. Guys. Now you're just being ridiculous. Put the wine skins down and work with me here," said Reuben.

"I know!" exclaimed Gad.

"What do you know?" asked Reuben. "You've never had an original thought in your life."

Dismissing Reuben's snub, Gad went on, "We could say that a wild beast attacked Joseph, and we were too late to save him. So we buried his body here in the desert. We could slaughter a sheep, and dip Joseph's coat in blood as proof of his demise."

The brothers looked at each other in turn, astonished at the plausibility of the idea, and agreed that this made a lot more sense than the circus. Just as they had finished their plans, a caravan of Ishmaelites approached. Providence was to provide a better way.

The brothers retrieved Joseph from the well and sold him to the shrewd band of exceedingly hairy camel traders for 20 pieces of silver. The die was cast. The dirty deed was done. Now it was time to go home and perpetrate a colossal hoax on their father.

When Israel heard the news and saw the bloody robe, he became distraught and went into deep mourning. When they saw their father's tears, they were ashamed and sorry. Not sorry enough to confess, however. They tried to console themselves with the knowledge that at least they hadn't killed Joseph outright, although that was their original intent.

---

*Shorthand for "Officer of the Most Excellent Order of the British Empire," an honorary pat on the back to civilians who do something notable that brings honor to the realm.

AΩ

CHAPTER 10

THE BURNING BUSH
(From Exodus 3)

Moses sat awkwardly on the hillside beneath Mount Horeb, minding the sheep belonging to his father-in-law Jethro. His behind grew numb from lack of circulation. The forlorn sheep bleated randomly.

Moses chewed idly on what he thought was a piece of straw. However, it turned out to be no ordinary add-mud-and-water-to-make-a-brick straw. This was magic straw. After a time, the hallucinogenic properties of this excellent plant had worked their way through Moses. Not only could he not feel his bottom, but he couldn't feel the rest of his body either. "Well, this is fun," he thought. "Oh, look! A bunny."

Just at that moment, and entirely without provocation, a nearby juniper bush burst majestically into flames. Moses remained seated on the Horeb hillside, calmly watching the bush burn. Moses had no idea how long he stared into the crackling flames, but it finally dawned on him that although the shrub was ablaze, it was not consumed.

"Amazing! I wonder how that works?" Moses mused, fantasizing about roasting marshmallows on this endlessly renewable energy source. As soon as Moses stood up to inspect the smokeless vegetation, the Lord God called out to him from the depths of the flickering flames: "Moses?! Is that you?"

This seemed patently absurd because, well, God, being God, already knew exactly to whom he was speaking. Perhaps the address was just a polite formality.

"Yo! Here I am!" declared Moses, leaning just a bit to the right.

"Keep your distance, and take off your Birkenstocks," said the fire, "for this is holy ground."

Now this frightened Moses, because he had been tending Jethro's sheep for a long time and had never considered the venue sacred. Recalling a time when he had taken a luxurious piss not far from the talking shrub raised his anxiety level exponentially. So Moses hid his face because he was embarrassed. But God, seemingly oblivious to his discomfort, continued outlining the divine unfolding without missing a beat.

AΩ

"I have observed the suffering of my people under the yoke of the Egyptians," said God. "And BTW, what is it with you people—seriously? This slavery thing is going to come up again and again. You're a lazy lot. Do your own work for my sake. You can't 'own' each other. It's a violation of the contract.

"But I digress. You will go to Pharaoh under my aegis and demand that the people be released. Then you will lead them through the land of the Canaanites and the Parasites to the place which I will show you."

Moses, resisting the overwhelming urge to take a leak, that particular necessity still being much on his mind, put his sandals back on, took up his crook, and began to herd the grazing sheep toward home, wondering how he would ever explain his vision to his wife Zipporah without appearing too stoned.

He decided en route to keep quiet. If he could not satisfactorily account for the last few hours, even to himself, then what chance did he have with her? He loved her madly—mostly—but she had a suspicious nature.

Oh, look. Another bunny.

Amy Adams Squire

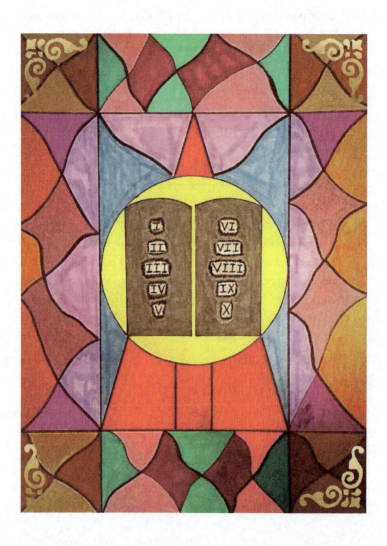

AΩ

CHAPTER 11

TO DON'T LIST
(From Exodus 20)

Moses, now the newly consecrated leader of the Israelites, was the only person allowed to scale Mount Sinai to visit God. Because the mountain was constantly enveloped in smoke and lightning—both signs of a superpower in the vicinity—no one but Moses was very keen to go up anyway. So that worked out.

Generally, Moses and God just had coffee and shot the breeze for about an hour. But today was a business meeting, and attendance was mandatory.

"Look, Moses," said God, shaking his head. "You have got to get a grip on these people. They are like second-graders jacked up on Gummy Bears. They smart off to you, break their toys, give each other wedgies, and steal pencils from the supply cabinet."

"I know. I know, Lord," said Moses, putting his head in his hands. "What's a prophet to do?"

"Relax," said God. "I have a cunning plan." God whipped out his easel dry-erase board and said, "Now, moving forward, take notes. For some reason, you all need enumerations to live by: the twelve steps, the eight-fold path, the four agreements,

29

and so on. I have condensed human morality into the following ten talking points, which, by the way, Moses, are for you too.

1. "There are a lot of deities and demi-divines roaming the universe. I've sent a secure email to everyone to let them know that humankind is an endearing species in its own way, but that you are not really Mensa material. No offense, but you do get confused easily. That's my fault, I suppose. In any case, henceforth, you shall have no other gods before me. I got you out of Egypt, no small feat I can tell you. Therefore, I take primacy over all other gods.

2. "No more graven images. Stop making idols that look like animals. You look ridiculous bowing before a cow, a cat, a bird, or a fish.

3. "Swearing is right out, especially taking my name in vain."

At this point, Moses interjected, saying, "Not to put too fine a point on it, Lord, but when I asked you what your name was, you replied, 'I AM THAT I AM,' which sounds very grand when you're bellowing it out of a belching mountain, but basically it was your way of saying, 'It's none of your beeswax.' How can I take a name in vain that has not yet been given to me?"

"Hmm. Fair point," said God. "Okay. How 'bout this then. However you refer to me, show some respect."

"Done," agreed Moses.

4. "Don't disregard the Sabbath. You could've had seven days to fart around, but you ruined that. So I saved you one day, different from all the others, set apart. Keep it holy and use it to reflect on my great mercy and rest from your labors. Have some fun. Go to the movies.

"Can do," said Moses.

5. "Don't disrespect your mother and father.

"Before you get all whiny and argumentative, Moses, let me just acknowledge that breeding does not confer maturity. I've seen the way you people parent. Yeesh. I don't have a dysfunctional family; I have a dysfunctional chosen people.

"The point here is that even if your parents are selfish and impatient, they deserve some latitude because they are doing the very best they can with what they've got.

6. "I wrote this one with you particularly in mind, Moses, Don't murder anyone—at least not on purpose. As for abortion, capital punishment, and death with dignity, work those issues out for yourselves. I can't do everything for you. Just bear in mind that essentially, it's not cost-effective for me to create life just to have you snuff it out.

7. "You shall not commit adultery. Perhaps some clarification is needed here as well. Sex is a good thing. It's fun. It feels good. It produces children. It is life-affirming when used in its proper context. If you run around banging each other's partners, you violate sacred trusts, which destroys a community. And just a medical footnote, indiscriminate shagging can also put you at risk for some really uncomfortable STDs.

8. "Don't steal. This should be self-explanatory.

9. "Do not bear false witness against your neighbor. Here we see the law of karma at her most precise. You make up some crap about your neighbor, and Lady Karma will throw it right back at you—times ten!

10. "I had a long version of this, but suffice it to say, don't covet anything you see or anyone you meet. This breeds selfishness and crime. You become obsessed with the object of your jealousy, and soon an idol has replaced me in your heart. And we're right back to where we started: Thou shalt have no other gods before me."

Amy Adams Squire

AΩ

CHAPTER 12

BABYLONIAN IDOL
(From Exodus 32)

Moses was away having another tête-à-tête with God on the mountain. They debated some of the finer points of the Decalogue, which took considerable time. At the conclusion of their conclave, God wrote the final draft in his own hand and set it in stone.

Meanwhile in the valley below, the unwashed masses grew anxious, fearing something bad had happened to Moses because he was gone so long. Maybe God had kidnapped him. The Israelites still harbored something of that learned helplessness from their days of bondage in Egypt. They couldn't function autonomously. They did better if they had a law to live by and a leader to interpret it for them.

When Moses failed to return in a timely manner, the people went to Moses' older brother Aaron. They beseeched Aaron to make for them an idol like the ones they remembered from Egypt. Aaron was a good guy, but having lived with the embarrassment of being overshadowed by his younger brother, he lacked a certain mettle and was never comfortable with being left at the helm.

Aaron relented and told the people to bring all their gold to him. A big, shiny calf was fashioned from the smelted gold, and the people partied like it was 1999. Take any large group of restless, fertile people, add alcohol and a graven image, and you've got yourself the makings of a first-rate orgy.

They ate, they drank, they sang karaoke, they danced, and they shagged. The ruckus was deafening.

Eventually, the racket reached the ear of God, who was more than a little incensed. The Almighty threatened all manner of retribution against the people whom he had rescued from their sad plight in Egypt. "This . . . this is how they thank me?" God sputtered.

Moses pleaded with God. "Look. I know they're a fickle lot, but they're my fickle lot. Besides, you're not doing yourself any favors acting like a maniac."

"Fine. Fine," said God, throwing up his hands. "Just know this: if you don't deal with them, I will." Nobody wanted that.

When Moses finally reached the foot of the mountain and beheld the folly of the Israelites, he was positively apoplectic. Throwing the Sinai Bible to the ground, Moses stormed through the wreckage in search of Aaron with every intention of giving him a righteous earful. Moses found Aaron snoring under a hamper with a bong in his hand. "GET UP! You good-for-nothing sonuva no-hump camel!" shouted Moses, giving Aaron a swift kick in his manly parts.

Aaron opened one eye and groaned.

"What made you think this was a good idea?" asked Moses, hands on hips. From the angle at which Aaron was lying, Moses reminded him of their mother.

AΩ

"The people were afraid because you were gone so long, and they asked me to make an idol that they could worship in your absence."

"And if the people had asked you to run out into traffic, would you have done that too? You're the older brother. I left you in charge. WTF? Now all the neighboring tribes are laughing at us for our faithlessness. God is hopping mad.

"The people have committed a great sin. Clean this mess up and gather the people together so that they may repent, while I go see if there is some atonement I may make to God on behalf of your sorry ass."

Aaron began collecting the empties. Moses put on his climbing sandals and headed back up the mountain, because he knew better than anyone that with God you just have to be persistent.

CHAPTER 13

WE ARE FAMILY
(From The Book of Ruth)

One constant in ancient times was famine, and it is in this context that we begin our story of how to be creative when it comes to family.

In the days when the judges* ruled, there was a famine in the land. So a man by the name of Elimelech and his wife Naomi took their two sons to the country of Moab, presumably to find work and food.

The Bible is unclear about cause of death, but in their new home in Moab, Elimelech died. Naomi's sons each married Moabite women. One was named Orpah (not to be confused with Oprah, the talk show host), and the other was named Ruth. After about ten years, both of Naomi's sons died. Again, cause of death, undisclosed. That happens a lot in the Bible.

Without the requisite males to provide her with status or protection, Naomi took her beloved daughters-in-law by the hand and bid them return to their own people.

AΩ

Orpah bailed tout suite, but Ruth refused to leave her, for she loved Naomi very much and was fiercely loyal to her. This meant that Ruth would have to leave her own land of Moab and settle in Judea, a foreign land, involving some culture shock, not unlike moving from Boulder to Biloxi. Without a husband for either woman, it would in all likelihood mean a life of poverty.

So Ruth and Naomi left the plateau of Moab and returned to Bethlehem. They arrived around April, just as the barley harvest was about to commence, a good omen for sure.

Care for the poor and the stranger was an integral part of Jewish life. Something we moderns could definitely learn a lesson from. It was common for those with means to allow the poor to follow in the wake of the threshers and gather up the remnants of grain.

In Bethlehem, Naomi had a prominent relative from her late husband's clan. His name was Boaz, and he was a hardworking, righteous man, and, although older than Ruth, was fit, prosperous, and, most importantly, unattached.

Long story short: because of Ruth's fidelity to Naomi and Boaz's generosity to Ruth, Ruth and Boaz married and had a son whom they named Obed. Obed became the father of Jesse and the grandfather of David. This would prove to be an auspicious lineage.

People who profess to embrace only the model of marriage found in the Bible should definitely consider this model of fidelity and creativity. You love those who have loved you or who need your love, and you navigate a convoluted social structure until it works out.

---

*The judges were a series of rulers or military leaders who functioned as ad hoc chieftains to the tribes of Israel in times of trouble and in the absence of a centralized government.

CHAPTER 14

BEAUTY AND THE BEAST
(From 1 Samuel 16.14-19; 17)

SAUL

Our story begins with the powerful Israelite King Saul. Apparently, Saul would periodically succumb to bouts of depression, maybe even paranoia. What king doesn't get paranoid, right? I'm sure the DSM-5* has a category for his affliction. Back in the day, however, before every feeling and behavior was given a label and a corresponding medication, people just chalked up emotional lability to "an evil spirit."

Oliver Sacks** notwithstanding, one thing we think we've discovered in modern times that the ancients already understood quite well is the power of music to influence feeling. So one of King Saul's servants, who was worried about his king as well as his own job security, brought a skilled harp player to ease Saul's melancholy.

DAVID

The harpist was none other than David, the hero of our story. David was the son of Jesse of Bethlehem (a number of famous names came out of Bethlehem). In addition to being a

AΩ

humble shepherd, David was also a capable warrior, musician, and poet. It was also said that he was quite handsome, and as Hollywood has shown us, a pretty face will open a lot of doors.

David was sent for, and Jesse made a gift to the King of five loaves of bread, some homemade wine, a kid from the flock, and, of course, his son David.

David's expertise with the strings offered Saul relief from the depression. Saul became quite fond of David and decided to keep him, like a pet. King Saul made David his armor-bearer, and all was relatively copacetic until the Philistines showed up.

THE PHILISTINES

The Philistines were a people who originated in the Aegean region, and arrived and settled in the land now known as Palestine just about the same time as the Israelites. As has been true throughout human history, turf wars abounded. Sometimes I wonder if dudes have these pissing contests because they're bored and need something exciting to do. But what can be so appealing about having your head run through with a sword? Testosterone in excess can be a terrible thing. But I digress.

GOLIATH

The Philistines were ready to take the Israelites' land. They had rallied the troops and drawn their battle line. So Saul and the Israelites established base camp across the valley from them.

The Philistines chose Goliath of Gath, their most ferocious champion, to engage the foe. Clearly, Goliath—more beast than man really—was not to be trifled with. By today's reckoning, he stood 6'6" tall, an astonishing height by the average of the time. He was by all estimations about 300 lb. He was ensconced head-to-toe in bronze armor. His bronze helmet had a vicious looking

39

Kaiser-Wilhelm spike on top and a long nose guard, obscuring the view his face. A razor-sharp scimitar hung from his waist, which he was careful to hang facing outward when walking.

Preceded by his shield-bearer Patsy (thank you, Monty Python) and indifferent to his own enormous size and the crushing weight of his armor, Goliath strode effortlessly—javelin in hand—to the battle line at the edge of the vale.

His voice boomed like thunder as he taunted the Israelite forces, "Why do you come in riot gear? I don't see no riot here!" He laughed heartily, obviously amused by his own wit.

"My commander does not wish to attack unless it is necessary. So he has sent me out first. I don't want to brag (which meant that he did), but I am the bravest and the fittest of all the Philistine soldiers. Send the best of your puny ranks to spar with me. The winner shall take the losing forces into servitude."

The Israelites knew they were screwed. There was none among the ranks as imposing as this bad boy.

David's position in King Saul's army was sort of auxiliary, something akin to the National Guard. David went to Saul and said, "Your Majesty, before I came to you, I was a shepherd. I have killed both lions and bears to protect my sheep. Grant that this day I may take down Goliath. He is an uncircumcised idolater, and his people have insulted the army of the living God. The Lord has always protected me and will do so again."

"Go with my blessing," replied Saul. "I want you to take my own sword and wear my armor for protection and advantage."

This command was one of those ideas that was lauded in the staff meeting but did not play out well in actuality. David looked like Harry Potter lost in his cousin Dudley's hand-me-downs. Swimming in metal and unable to take a step without swaying under the weight, David removed the armor and told the king that because he was unaccustomed to the gear, it would

AΩ

be a hindrance. Saul agreed, took an aspirin, and laid down in his tent for a bit.

David said his prayers, took up his staff, and selected five smooth stones and put them in a bag with his sling. Then he advanced to meet the enormous Philistine.

As David drew nearer to Goliath, Goliath, who was severely myopic, squinted to see whom the Israelites had sent to his death. Because of Goliath's near-sightedness, David looked like a woman coming towards him. Goliath doubled over with laughter, howling until his sides hurt. Goliath exclaimed, "WTF!? His Royal Majesty Saul has lost his mind! He sends a woman to fight the mighty Goliath?!" As David drew nearer still, Goliath saw that David was but a youth, handsome and ruddy.

Then Goliath swore by all his gods, and he had quite a collection. "You little toe-rag! I'll leave you to rot for vulture food!"

David replied, "You come at me with sword and spear, but I come against you in the Name of the Lord of Hosts."

As Goliath advanced on him, David took out his sling and a stone and hurled it. The stone struck the behemoth squarely in the unprotected space above his brow like a missile. Goliath dropped to his knees and fell forward, dead, the rock imbedded in his forehead. David ran over, and using Goliath's own sword, cut off his head and held it up for all to see.

The Philistines ran away in disbelief and terror. The Israelites cheered and jumped up and down, slapping each other on the back.

Score one for team Jehovah!

Diagnostic and Statistical Manual of Mental Disorders, ed. 5
**Author of *Musicophilia*, a groundbreaking work exploring the effects of music on neural pathways.

CHAPTER 15

BEL AND EL
(From Job 1 and 2)

Bel* was a theomorph who roamed the earth, appearing in the likeness of various desert deities, depending on his mood or mission. Bel had been unceremoniously banished from heaven by El** for the crime of refusing to pay homage to Adam, prototype of the two-leggeds. How could any ranking member

AΩ

of the celestial order deign to pay tribute to a subpar species? Bel was made of stardust. Adam was made of dirt.

Biding his time, waiting for the right moment to exact revenge for such a gross indignity, Bel saw his chance to give the proverbial one-digit salute to El by bringing God's favored servant Job to his knees.

Job dwelt in the land of Uz (not to be confused with Oz—another land where strange things happened). Now Job was a righteous dude and a standup guy by anyone's standards. He was also a bazillionaire, owning vast tracks of land, herds of livestock, and mutual funds. He was the patriarch of an unusually prolific family who occupied many tents.

One day Bel adopted his most pathetic expression and went to El, saying, "I am weary of wandering the earth, which, by the way, is no paradise. It's a proper dump."

"Well, whose fault is that?" asked El.

"Fair point," conceded Bel, trying to move the conversation along. "I have been much impressed by your boy Job. He is pious and faithful, but what if he were penniless? Would he still make prayers and sacrifices for himself and his children? It's easy to be committed when you have a backup plan."

El took a real-time moment to consider the proposal. Most of the two-legged creatures had been an epic fail. But Job was a diamond among the marbles. Perhaps it would be useful to know if Job would rise a champion if thrown to the mat.

"Deal," said El, "but with one condition."

"Can't you do anything without a caveat?" Bel whined. "It's like, here is this awesome garden, but you can't touch this tree."

El did not appreciate having his shortcomings pointed out to him. "One condition," he said stiffly. "You may smite Job, but you may not take his life. Only I give life, and only I may take it."

"Done!" agreed Bel.

43

And so began the afflictions of Job.

First, Bel launched guided missiles at Job's flocks of sheep, obliterating them in one huge inferno. Next Bel sent roving hordes of unkempt, toothless Chaldeans who made off with Job's camels. Then came the tornado, which blew through the Uz Trailer Park, scattering Job's offspring to the four corners of the earth. Finally came the trial that brought Job right up to the line between life and death. The piéce de résistance. Bel ravaged Job's body with the pox. Not just any old pox either. This was smallpox, the pox of poxes.

Poor Job became a broken man, overcome with grief and covered in sores. He tore his clothes and wept bitterly. He shaved his head (and not very expertly) and sat alone among the ruins of his life. But in all this he did not accuse or question El. At last, his wife came to him—keeping a discreet distance for fear of the plague. "So, Mr. Holier-Than-Thou. You—WE—have been royally shat on. No one would blame you if you cursed God and packed it in."

"My dear," replied Job patiently, "The Lord giveth, and the Lord taketh away. Blessed be the name of the Lord."

Job's wife went away shaking her head and mumbling to herself, "Oh, right! Blessed be the name of the Lord. I think I'll just run right out and build an altar to the god who just made my home a crater."

El made a mental note to be patient with Job's wife and to restore Job's blessings a hundredfold.

---

*Bel, a title rather than a name, used for a variety of Mesopotamian gods, usually competing for primacy.

**El, the Semitic name of the supreme God.

AΩ

CHAPTER 16

ERRAND BOY
(From the Book of Jonah)

The ancients had a curious relationship with God. They talked to God; God talked back. God sent them on errands on his behalf. If they failed, God smote them. If they succeeded, God blessed them. The people were fickle, and God was mercurial. The relationship between God and the people was mutual but oddly dysfunctional. The plight of Jonah illustrates this unusual relationship rather neatly.

Apparently, God had had his eye on the city of Ninevah for some time. The residents were prone to partying, debauchery, and mischief. What to do?

God decided to enlist the help of his good friend Jonah. "Jonah, son of the prophet Amittai," bellowed God from the heavens. "Go to the city of Nineveh and preach against them. Tell them to repent of their sins and return to me."

Jonah was having none of it. He went down to Joppa and hopped on the first ship sailing for anywhere away from the Lord, which happened to be Tarrshish.

This put God in a right state. So he conjured up a mighty storm that bashed the boat around like a double-wide trailer in a tornado. The various deities of the region were beseeched to come to the aid of the floundering vessel, without success. So the sailors tossed the ship's cargo overboard in hopes of lightening the load. Meanwhile, Jonah lay napping in his bunk below deck, oblivious to the maelstrom above.

The captain found Jonah asleep and woke him with a smack on the head, saying, "What the are you doing snoring like a hog at this hour? We are drowning! Get your sorry ass out of bed and call upon your God to save us."

The ancients, not unlike us moderns, were a superstitious lot. So they played dice to divine who among the passengers had caused this disaster. The lots fell on Jonah. So the crew interrogated him: Who are you? Where do you come from? Who are your people? What is your business on this ship?

"I am a Hebrew," Jonah answered. I worship the Lord, the God who made both the sea and the dry land. But I am running away. So throw me overboard because it is on my account that the Lord's wrath has been stirred up."

"You don't have to ask us twice," said the captain. And the men chucked Jonah over the side of the boat and into the raging ocean.

Rather than let Jonah drown, God sent a ginormous fish to swallow him up. And Jonah lived in the belly of the creature for three days and three nights, which gave him plenty of timeout to consider the error of his ways. Now, how one could remain calm enough to compose poetry while living in the digestive tract of a sea monster defies plausibility. However, from his meditation, Jonah composed the following prayer:

Out of my distress, I called to the Lord, and he answered me.

AΩ

From the midst of the nether world, I cried for help, and you heard my voice.

For you cast me into the deep, into the heart of the sea, and the flood enveloped me. Fear consumed me. Seaweed clung to my head. I became jetsam.

But you, my God, saved me, and I praise your Name for my deliverance.

With that, the great fish, finding human flesh most distasteful, barfed up poor Jonah on the shore.

And so, the Word of the Lord came to Jonah a second time. God is nothing if not persistent, a nag when it comes right down to it. This time Jonah obeyed, knowing that running around Ninevah pronouncing judgment like a lunatic was preferable to being made into fish food on the high seas.

Ninevah was a thriving metropolis, so large that it took three days to walk through. Jonah put on his sandwich board, which read "THE END IS NEAR," and walked through the city announcing that Ninevah had a drop-dead date of 40 days to change their unrighteousness ways before God would take them out.

Amazingly, the people of Ninevah believed Jonah, and they fasted and repented. They returned to their original spouses, gave back stolen goods, made amends for lies told, paid their delinquent taxes, and generally cleaned up their act.

When the King of Ninevah heard what was happening, he went into mourning mode and proclaimed a citywide fast. And when God saw their remorse—even that of their king—he spared them.

CHAPTER 17

UNPLANNED PARENTHOOD
(From Luke 1.26-56)

IT'S A GIRL!

Mary, the only child of Anna and Joachim, was expected to be a boy who would be dedicated to service in the Temple. But with God's customary flair for blindsiding the species who thought they knew everything, God produced a lively, dark-haired baby girl. At her naming ceremony, Joachim pronounced her "Miriam." She would become the holy Temple in which the Messiah would be conceived.

Mary was a precocious child, compassionate and courageous. She grew into a self-possessed young woman who was unusually and fiercely devoted to God. Although Mary's

AΩ

devout nature often took her outside the accepted social and religious limitations of her gender, her parents wisely allowed her the latitude to explore her mystic nature because they realized that God had a special plan and purpose for her. Little did they know.

As was the custom of the time, Mary's parents arranged for her to marry at the age of fifteen. Her intended was Joseph Bar Nun, fifteen years her senior. Women mature much more quickly than men, and the pool of responsible, pious, young men was but a puddle. So Mary's parents approached the quiet, hardworking, righteous widower to be the husband of their precious daughter. Joseph agreed without hesitation.

THE ANNUNCIATION

In the month of Elul, God sent Gabriel, one of his seven trusty archangels, to reveal to Mary her part in the divine unfolding. She had to accept first, of course. With God, you always get options.

One sweltering afternoon, Mary was leaning against a small fig tree near the well from which she had just drawn water. Taking comfort from its meager shade, she began to doze. Suddenly, she was aware that the shade had expanded, as if a shadow had fallen over her. She started, thinking she had fallen asleep and the sun was setting. Upon opening her eyes, she saw a magnificent winged creature standing over her. He stood on two legs like a man but was nearly four heads taller than any man she had ever seen. Although the being appeared to stand upright, he also seemed to not be touching the ground at all.

Seeing her terrified expression (quite common to mortals experiencing the celestial order for the first time), Gabriel tried to reassure Mary that he meant her no harm. "Fear not!" said Gabriel in his most convincing tone.

"Fear not?! Are you insane?!" cried Mary. "I'm looking at a giant butterfly!"

"Yes, well, I am sort of imposing," Gabriel agreed. "But I mean you no harm." Mary's skepticism registered in her expression almost audibly.

"I bring you a message from the Lord of Hosts," said Gabriel, trying to get to the point.

"Is that right? What could be so important that you have to frighten me half to death?"

"You have been favored by God," said Gabriel. Mary crossed her arms over her chest. "You have been favored by God," Gabriel began again, "and chosen to carry the seed of God himself. You will conceive and bear a son whom you will name Jesus. And he will save the people from their sins." Gabriel felt relieved to have gotten it all out this time.

"I'm a virgin, not an idiot. I haven't had intimate relations with Joseph—or anyone else for that matter—and just like that, abracadabra, I'm pregnant?"

Gabriel agreed that she had a solid argument. So he explained in greater detail, something he was prepared to do but had hoped to avoid. "The Holy Spirit will come upon you, and the essence of the Most High will overshadow you. Nothing is impossible with God," explained Gabriel.

"I have been dedicated to God since my birth. Difficult decisions won't change that. So then let it be to me according to your word."

Having secured the much sought-after response, Gabriel took his leave, knowing that Creation was about to change irrevocably and permanently.

AΩ

CHAPTER 18

BORN IN A BARN
(From Matthew 1; Luke 2)

When the Angel Gabriel told Mary she would become a mother, he also told her that she was to name the child Jesus. Mary had favored the name Roger, but Gabriel was most insistent. After Mary learned that she was indeed pregnant, she took a little road trip to visit a relative named Elizabeth who lived in the Judean boondocks.

Coincidentally, Elizabeth was also pregnant. The two had a great time knitting baby things, having tea, and talking about whatever it is that pregnant women talk about.

Not long after Mary returned home, Joseph, her intended, packed up the mules and said, "Hop on. We're going to Bethlehem for the census."

"Oh, sure," said Mary. "There is nothing I'd rather do than ride a donkey to Timbuktu while I'm eight-and-a-half months pregnant. My ankles are swollen and I have to pee every 20 minutes. I hope Governor Quirinius appreciates the effort." (You may surmise correctly that it was from his mother that Jesus inherited his wry wit.)

So off they went from Nazareth to Bethlehem, a distance of about 100 miles. When they arrived at their destination, Mary was dilated about five centimeters. No time to lose. Joseph parked the mules and ran to the first Shady Cedars Motel he could find.

"I'm sorry for your missus, bro," said the manager sympathetically, "but with the census and the Shriner's convention and all, we're overbooked already. Tell you what, though. I've got an outbuilding on the back forty. Settle in there, and I'll send the wife down ASAP with some supplies. No charge. Seeing as how it's special circumstances and all."

So Joseph took Mary, who was sweating and cramping, and they went in frantic search of the cowshed. He tried valiantly to reassure her that all would be well.

As Mary dismounted, she said those three words that strike terror in the heart of every man: My water broke.

The innkeeper's wife Madge arrived, as if on cue, with towels, blankets, food, and water. The mules had been hitched to a post outside the barn. One mule said to the other, "They call this a blessed event."

To which the other mule replied, "Blessed event, my eye! I'm drenched."

At that moment the lusty cry of a human baby came from inside the barn. The mules looked at each other and bowed their heads.

ΑΩ

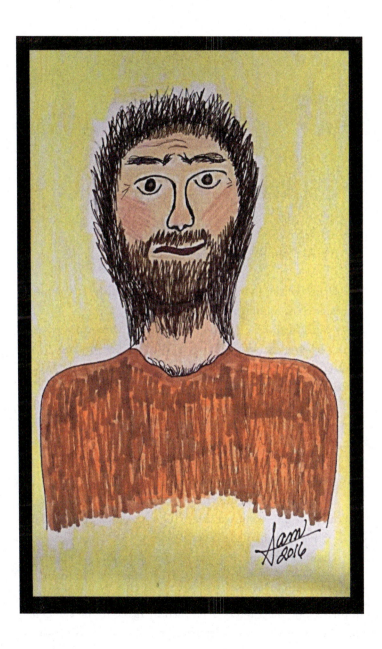

CHAPTER 19

SHALL WE GATHER AT THE RIVER?
(From Matthew 3.1-13; Luke 3.1-22)

Jesus' cousin, John, was that rare and peculiar amalgamation of madman, monastic, mystic, and martyr.

John's birth was heralded in much the same way as Jesus' birth, by angelic announcement. At his bar mitzvah, John realized that God had a special ministry for him. So like his cousin, Jesus, John also had received a nod from the Almighty, which caused some competition between the boys. Even when they grew older, John was not much given to waiting in the wings while Jesus ran around doing his messiah thing, showing off his smarts for the rabbis and playing parlor tricks with the loaves and fishes.

In the end, however, they would both piss off enough important people to be executed. John would be beheaded, and Jesus would be crucified. There's no funny in that.

The Roman Emperor Tiberius had been on the throne for fifteen years when the Word of God came to Elizabeth and Zechariah's only son John. At that time, John was living rough in the desert. He could be identified by his ill-fitting camel hair tunic, accented by a worn leather belt. John was also known by his penchant for raw food, primarily locusts and wild honey. Blech! What's wrong with a nice roasted quail now and again?

John's expectations of himself and his demands on others were rigorous to say the least. He ran around Jordan as an itinerant preacher, raving about the baptism of repentance, whatever that was. "'I am the voice of one crying out in the wilderness,'" John shouted, quoting the prophet Isaiah.

"Yeah. The wilderness of your own deranged mind," said the people around him, shaking their heads.

The Pharisees took umbrage at his preaching and declared, "We have the law of Moses and Abraham as our father. What need have we of repentance or this baptism of which you speak?"

Disregarding their disdain for him, John cried, "You tangled brood of pit vipers! Sons of the sons of serpents, with your rigid, tiny reptile minds. Who told you that you would be spared the wrath to come?"

Most people assumed John to be either drunk or mentally unbalanced, or maybe just a little stoned around the edges. But there were many among the throng who were able to look past John's bizarre demeanor and discern the truth of his words. It was they who asked him what they should do.

"Bear fruit worthy of repentance," he answered. "Let go of your parsimonious ways and share joyfully with those in need. Confess your dishonesty, repent of your extortion, and disavow your licentiousness. Instead, embrace fidelity. Live simply. Pray for peace. Grant forgiveness. When you have done these things in your heart, be baptized here with the waters of the Jordan River as a sign of your intention to amend your lives with God's help."

Sadly, but predictably, it was the common people of no particular import who were already close enough to the kingdom of heaven to desire rebirth. One by one, soldiers, tax collectors, and shepherds stepped into the muddy waters and allowed John to submerge them. They came up out of the water renewed and radiant.

The wealthy and the highly placed, however, put their noses in the air, turned on their heels, and walked away defiant and sanctimonious. And thus has it always been.

AΩ

CHAPTER 20

YOU HAVE NO POWER HERE
(From Matthew 4)

After Jesus had been baptized by John in the River Jordan, he was drenched. Thinking to dry himself out, he went into the desert a ways and sat in the sun. The Spirit of God told him that before he could do any good work, he must first be awakened. So Jesus promptly lay down under a cliff and took a nap.

While he slept, Jesus dreamed that he had been wandering in the desert like his ancestors, for 40 days and 40 nights. After such a protracted period, Jesus was parched and starving. He continued to drift through the dunes, searching for sustenance. At length, the Tempter and Deceiver of the World appeared and said, "Well, well. If it isn't my old nemesis about to expire from malnutrition. Guess I got here just in time."

"Oh, what do you want, you old wanker? asked Jesus wearily.

"What do I want? Why nothing at all. I'm here to give you everything you could ever want."

"And what do you know about what I want?" Jesus replied.

The Tempter took out some hummus and pita bread and made a sandwich, which he ate in front of Jesus without offering him any. "I know," said the Tempter, taking a large bite and

57

talking with his mouth full, "that you want to save the whole world. Don't you?"

Jesus nodded.

"Well, first of all, you can't save the people from their sins on an empty stomach. Jesus reached for the sandwich, but the Tempter held it back. "Oh, no, no, no, my friend. Is the Son of God too pathetic to fend for himself?" The Tempter arranged some stones in a circle and said, "Turn these stones into bread. You know you want to."

Jesus shook his head, "If I am the Son of God, how could mere bread nourish me? Only the true Word from the mouth of God can sustain me."

"Fine," said the Tempter, finishing his snack and brushing the crumbs from his cargo pants. "So you're going to save the whole world on a diet. Whatever. But how are you going to redeem creation as an itinerant preacher. Hmmm? You need to think big, here, Jesus. Look at the larger picture, the greater good."

The Tempter took Jesus to the top of a mountain and said, "There! Cast your royal eye over the horizon and behold all the kingdoms of the earth, past, present, and yet to come. All these I will put within your grasp if you will renounce your birthright and become my partner and heir."

At once Jesus saw how he was being deluded and seduced. He turned to the Tempter and declared, "You brought my people to their knees, but I will raise them up. Be gone from my sight! You have no power here!"

The Tempter retreated, defeated but biding his time.

Jesus woke up, glad to be shot of the nightmare. Then the angels came and took care of him until he was ready to begin his work.

CHAPTER 21

JESUS TURNS PRO
(From John 2.1-11)

The wedding at Cana in Galilee was to be an exciting and eventful day for our hero Jesus of Nazareth. It would be the first public demonstration of His divine superpowers. His mother, predictably, acted as his promoter.

Jesus' BFF Lester and Lester's betrothed Bianca were getting ready to storm the chuppah. Mazel tovs all around!

After the ceremony, the steward in charge of the reception, which came complete with a bitchin' klezmer band and full buffet, went to Lester and said, "Um. Look, bro. Your guests are like sieves where liquor is concerned. The wine just runs right through them. Now, I'm ashamed to say, we're completely tapped."

Now Jesus' mother—like all mothers, especially Jewish and Italian mothers—had the hearing of a SETI antenna, and she overheard the panicked pronouncement. So she went to Jesus and said, "The steward has run out of wine. Be a good boy and get him some more—maybe something a little less corked."

Jesus rolled his eyes at her, and she thumped him in the head with her knuckles, saying "Is this how your treat the woman who gave you life?"

Jesus sighed. "Well, what would you like me to do? Run down to Costco? Besides, it is not yet time for me to reveal myself."

"Don't be cheeky. A mother always knows these things."

Mary left Jesus with his tipsy gaggle of frat-boy disciples and approached the head steward. "Look, my son is a little shy, but he can sort this out for you. Just do whatever he tells you. You won't be disappointed."

The steward had nothing to lose. It wasn't as if someone were going to turn water into wine for him. So he went to Jesus and said, "I hear you're a troubleshooter. There's ten denarii and a chicken in it for you if you can put this right."

"Keep your money," said Jesus. "But I will take the chicken. Now go fill those three huge jars to the brim with water."

The caterers looked at Jesus like deer caught in the headlights. "Tick tock!" The head steward barked, and the staff scampered away.

When the jars were full, Jesus instructed the steward to draw some water out and taste it. The wine steward, looking pale and

AΩ

sweaty, carefully sipped the water, which had now become an exquisite vintage. He was astounded. "Where did you get this fine wine?"

Jesus replied, "Don't look a gift horse in the mouth." Then Jesus turned around and walked away, a slight swagger in his gait.

Mary stood with the women and nodded approvingly. "My son the Messiah," she thought to herself.

CHAPTER 22

ATTITUDES
(From Matthew 5)

By this time, Jesus had organized a motley crew (not to be confused with the band) who became known as his disciples. There were actually about 25 charter members. These included Simon Peter, a blowhard fisherman; his brother Andrew, a quiet lad who lived in Peter's shadow; Matthew, a reformed IRS agent; Luke, a devout twenty-something who was clearly having issues with his sexual orientation; Mary Magdalene, a friend with special privileges who supported the troupe financially; and Phyllida, a comely matron who had a generous heart and provided much-needed comic relief.

Jesus' ministry as a bona fide itinerant preacher and faith healer in Galilee was now in full swing. He was casting out demons here and curing epileptics there. Despite the fact that social media would not appear for about 2000 years yet, news of Jesus' message of mercy and gifts of grace spread rapidly.

One day at the "Sunshine Gospel Mission" the local flotsam began to swell the tent. They arrived not only from Galilee but also from Jerusalem and Judea. Seeing the whopping great

AΩ

throng of people, Jesus said to his disciples, "Let's take this show on the road."

And off he went with the crowd limping after him. Jesus found a small mountain (or a large hill) and climbed it to gain acoustical advantage. Remember, this was a bygone era, long before amplifiers, microphone, monitors, big screens, mega churches, or Joel Osteen.

Jesus sat down, struck his most elegant double lotus position, and began to teach.

"You can receive no blessing until you lose the attitude," he began bluntly. The crowd looked at each other, not knowing if they should be offended. Before they could decide, Jesus moved swiftly on.

"The Father would bless you with all manner of abundance because he loves you, but your minds and hearts are closed to it.

"You think you are spiritually enlightened because you hear the Torah read in the Synagogue each Shabbat. Be humble enough to accept that you know nothing! Ask God to show you the right path. In the asking, you will find the Kingdom of Heaven.

"You believe you will get more by competing and conniving. But I assure you that you shall possess the earth and all that is in it by sharing what you have and being gracious to one another.

"Your hearts are full of envy and vengeance. You will never see God while you plot against all who slight you. Empty your heart of this pettiness."

At that moment, Jesus' glance fell upon a man standing slightly to his left a few paces away. The man was scratching his backside exuberantly, and Jesus wondered if all was not lost already.

63

"Finally, my friends, you have learned that the only way to fight injustice is just to fight. But truly I tell you, like attracts like. Violence does not stop violence. It only creates more.

"Instead, greet injustice with justice, and address injury with pardon. Those who make peace, regardless of their station, are the real children of God."

With that, Jesus stood up and began to descend the hill. Although the people regarded Jesus mostly as a stoner, they couldn't help pondering all that he had said.

AΩ

CHAPTER 23

THE FULL MEAL DEAL
(From Matthew 14.13-21; Mark 6.30-44)

Grieving over John the Baptist's beheading, Jesus set out in a small V-hull fishing boat to get some much-needed "me" time. Good luck with that, Mr. Messiah, because the 99% need some hand-holding. The crowd followed Jesus along the coast. Finally, he put in to shore, and having great compassion for the masses, and needing to refocus, he healed the sick among them.

As the afternoon shadows lengthened, the disciples (who were frequently concerned about where and when the next meal would be) said, "Rabbi, it is getting late. We are hungry, and the crowd is huge, and they have nothing to eat."

Jesus, still grieving, was not in the mood for their petty complaints. "What do I look like? The pizza delivery guy? Feed them yourselves."

"Oh, he's in another one of his bleedin' moods," whispered Simon Peter to Mary.

"You're standing three feet away," said Jesus. "I can hear you, you know."

Peter shrugged and made one of his few attempts to think independently. He found a young lad among the throng who was holding a basket of fish. Peter took it—almost without asking—and presented it to Jesus, like a cat laying a freshly caught mouse at his master's feet.

Jesus had matured a bit since the wedding at Cana. The novelty of turning one thing into another had subsided. He inspected the basket of protruding fish tails and found that it actually contained 4 1/2 loaves of day-old bread and 5 headless fish, which, judging by hue and aroma, clearly would not be fit for consumption within a couple hours' time.

Now this next bit is important if you are to understand the nature of Jesus at all. Instead of looking at the meager contents of the basket as inadequate to feed the multitude or pleading with God to magically turn it into more, he simply held the tightly woven basket aloft. Casting his eyes toward heaven, he prayed, "Father, thank you for these gifts of Mother Earth. May they be blessed."

The disciples took the basket and began to distribute its contents among the grateful crowd, and all were filled to capacity.

CHAPTER 24

ADVANCED LIFE-SAVING
(From Matthew 14.22-33; Mark 6.45-52)

After the picnic, the crowd went home at Jesus' behest. They probably would have stayed longer, but Jesus was a closet introvert. Despite his vocation, which required long periods with lots of people, he needed an inordinate amount of time alone. "The Happy Hermit," his friend Rachel once called him.

So off he went by himself to pray. The disciples couldn't figure out why praying in synagogue wasn't good enough, but Jesus had a habit of going up a mountain or down in the desert to commune with the divine.

So, his crew played pinochle on the boat while they waited for him. The game turned into an all-nighter. In the early hours, a storm was brewing, and they abandoned their games to keep the boat from capsizing.

Suddenly, they saw Jesus walking toward them—on the water!? They nearly crapped themselves with terror, assuming him to be a specter. Knowing how little faith and comprehension these guys could have, Jesus tried to calm them, "Chill. It's only me."

The retelling of stories about the early days had turned Thomas into the infamous doubter. It was always Peter, however, who consistently challenged Jesus to prove himself.

"Okay," said Peter cautiously, "If it's really you," he went on, growing bolder, "bid me come to you upon the water."

To this, Jesus replied, "What are you waiting for? Water wings?"

Peter was a mountain of a man and did not alight from the vessel with ease. But once up and out, he approached Jesus, walking upon the waves. All was well until Peter saw the wind roughing up the water beneath the heavy skies. Then he began to sink.

Jesus reached out and caught him, saying, "Fear will always cause you to drown."

AΩ

CHAPTER 25

GOOD AS NEW
(From John 11.1-44)

Jesus had quite an entourage going. Some were groupies. Some were disciples. Some were friends. Some were just curious. Among those who followed and supported his ministry was the Eleazar* family of Bethany, consisting of the three sibling survivors Mary, Martha, and Lazarus.

One day, quite unannounced, Lazarus became severely ill. Some said it was heatstroke. Some speculated that it was food poisoning. But whatever it was, Lazarus was in a very bad way: fever, chills, sweating, vomiting, and eventually loss of consciousness. Various bona fide physicians as well as their charlatan counterparts were sent for out of sheer desperation. However, none of these healers was able to produce even the slightest improvement in his condition.

Not really wanting Jesus to know he was the last resort, but having run out of options, Lazarus' sisters sent a message to Jesus asking him to come at once to heal their ailing brother. When Jesus received the message, he did not respond immediately. Using the opportunity to make a point, as messiahs are wont to do, Jesus said, "This illness is critical but is not fatal."

69

Amy Adams Squire

Knowing what was to come, Jesus stayed put for a couple days and prayed for his friend. After the sun had risen and set two times, Jesus rounded up the disciples, broke camp, and without so much as a by-your-leave announced that they were all going Judea. When Jesus and his band of merry misfits arrived, he discovered that Lazarus was already dead and buried. Shiva mourners filled the house.

Martha, the more extroverted of the two sisters, ran out to meet Jesus. In tears, she cried, "Oh, Jesus. Why didn't you come sooner? If you had been here, Lazarus would not have died." Jesus, much moved by the palpable grief around him, also began to cry.

Mary, who had remained in the house, as was her duty, finally came out and met Jesus. The mourners followed her. Mary upbraided Jesus, "What was so important that you couldn't come to see to Lazarus? Now he's dead. You are too late."

Jesus said to her, "Mary, I'm sorry, but have faith. Your brother lives. Where is the tomb?"

Mary took him to where they had laid Lazarus' body to rest. Jesus' moment of opportunity had come. He ordered some of the men to roll the stone away from the cave which held the body.

The crowd blanched. They stood motionless, staring at him as if he had just announced that camels could speak French.

"Whoa, there, dude!" exclaimed one of the mourners. "Not to be rude or anything, but Lazarus is four days gone now. Do you know what it's going to smell like in there?"

Jesus looked toward heaven and thanked God for hearing him and then motioned for the stone to be moved.

The men held their collective breath and gave the boulder a mighty shove. Jesus peered in and said in a loud voice, "Lazarus! Wake up! It's okay. You can come out."

AΩ

They waited.

With perfect equanimity, Jesus repeated the command, "Lazarus, come out!"

The crowd heard something stirring in the cave, and at last Lazarus came out, wearing his shroud. This is the stuff of Christopher Lee and Vincent Price horror movies: the undead wandering about the crypt in their burial wrappings. The crowd gasped in unison and took a step back.

"Clean him up," said Jesus, and everyone present was astounded at this man who could command even death.

Amy Adams Squire

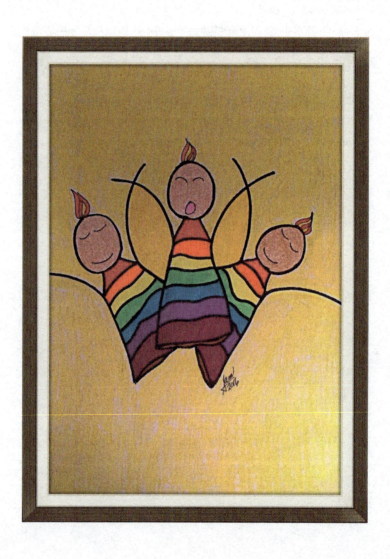

AΩ

CHAPTER 26

FIRE IN THE HOLE
(From Acts 1.23-26 -- 2.1-13)

The disciples played rock-paper-scissors to decide who would replace the turncoat Judas on the select committee. Best two out of three. Matthias won. The community having been restored, it was time to be commissioned to go into the world and spread the gospel of God's love in the person of Jesus the Christ.

When the day of Pentecost had come, women, men, young, old, Jew, and gentile, gathered together, filling the room to capacity. It was SRO that day. They held hands and entered into communal prayer. As they did this, the room suddenly filled with a heavenly light. No shadows anywhere, not even in the corners. It was as if the room itself had come alive. Then came a roar and the rush of a mighty wind that blew without moving so much as a hair on anyone's head. Neat trick, that. Some of the disciples were easily caught up in the mystery and the magic of the moment. Others glanced surreptitiously from side to side for a quick reality check.

About the time they thought there was going to be liftoff, the fire came. Individual flames like flickering candles appeared

73

over the heads of each person without singeing even a thread on anyone's robe. The whole place looked like the encore at a Neil Diamond concert. They were all filled with the power of the Holy Spirit, and, as a sign of this indwelling, they began to speak in other languages as the Spirit directed them.

Thus, a new religion was born—not that the world needed another religion, and not that Jesus had ever been interested in starting one. The time had come, however, for the redemption of the world from the fall of Adam and his descendants.

AΩ

CHAPTER 27

SAUL'S EXCELLENT ADVENTURE
(From Acts 9)

Saul of Tarsus was one of the blowhard brand of religious zealots like you see on TV, pounding his pulpit, waving the Torah, and getting hypertensive screaming about the sacrilege and perversion of the Christians. Most reasonable and mentally balanced Jews distanced themselves doctrinally—and physically, if possible—from Saul. He made it embarrassing to be Jewish.

It was hard to think of Saul as one of God's chosen people, unless he was chosen specifically for the task of showing everyone else what not to be like.

Saul and his sanctimonious brownshirts (note the special irony here) travelled from town to town ferreting out Christians, dragging them before the authorities, and stoning them to death.

Of course there was a legitimate reason to be wary of Christians. They were a rapidly expanding cult devoted to a man named Jesus. Jesus was executed by the Romans and was purported to have risen from the grave. That was some seriously crazy shit. What made the Christians so dangerous, however, was not their mythology but their mission statement: Do unto others as you would have them do unto you. That right there was the stuff of sedition. No more "an eye for an eye." Now it was "turn the other cheek." Start teaching that pacifistic, bleeding-heart nonsense, and it's the end of the world as we know it, which was, ironically, the point of such practices.

Saul had gone to the high priest to obtain warrants granting him authority to seek out people of The Way (Christians) from among the synagogues in Damascus and have them arrested and brought to trial in Jerusalem. Unusually pleased with himself (which is saying something), Saul, breathing hellfire, set off with his caravan of hoodlums and sycophants. It was a beautiful day to catch some fish-eating hand-holders. Kumbaya.

They were about two hours from Damascus when the sky suddenly grew restless and overcast. Without warning, a bolt of lightning rocketed out of a cloud and struck Saul right on the top of his bald pate, knocking him clean off his camel. In some sort of weird, mystical folie à deux, a voice heard by everyone present said, "Saul! Saul! Why do you persecute me?" At once, one of the camel drivers wet himself and then promptly fainted.

Saul lay face down in the dirt and mumbled, "Who are you?"

AΩ

"Stand up, so I can speak to you properly," commanded the voice.

Saul stood slowly, brushing himself off. He supposed that he must have gotten a snootful of sand for he could see nothing but darkness. Again Saul asked, "Who are you?!"

The voice replied, "I am Jesus the Christ whom you persecute."

"Well, that's convenient," said Saul, beginning to find his bearings. "A disembodied voice from the sky that knocks me down and strikes me blind. Show yourself, you coward!"

Feisty one, that Saul. Gets thrashed by a deity and still has the cojones to go the distance. Fearing they had incurred God's displeasure, Saul's companions led poor, blind, and confused Saul on to Damascus to the house of Ananias, a disciple of Jesus.

And there Saul waited helplessly for three days to receive his sight again.

Amy Adams Squire

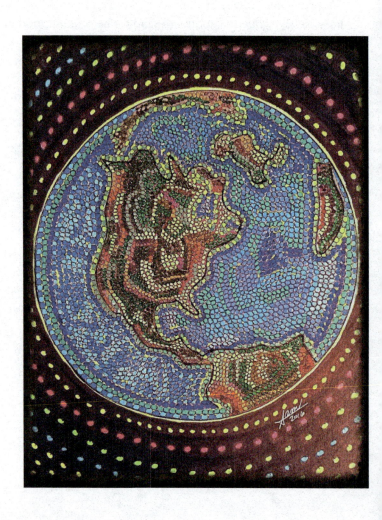

ΑΩ

CHAPTER 28

THE GRAND FINALE
(From the Revelation of John)

The author of our final fantasy is John. John had been exiled to the Greek Island of Patmos during a massive anti-Christian persecution undertaken by the Roman emperor Domitian. Boredom in exile can do strange things to a man's mind. What better way to occupy oneself in solitary and to ensure an enduring legacy than to pen an epic book of prophecy?

Incidentally, Revelation also has proved highly lucrative to writers who have followed down the ages. The authors of the Left Behind series LaHaye and Jenkins made a meal of it. If you want to make the big bucks, Jesus is the Way!

One very important theme in this saga is the idea of completing the circle of time and life. This is critical in most religions, particularly Paganism. Christianity stole just about everything from the Pagans: dying and resurrecting god, god born in a barn or cave, virgin birth, holidays, and sacred sites.

MAGICAL, MYSTICAL MISSIVES

The beginning of the end begins with letters to the seven churches in Asia. If you're going to reach out and touch someone, think globally. John tells the churches that the particulars of his missives were from a vision that an angel commanded him to write. One of the nice things about referencing an angel is that if the project fails, the angel is a convenient fall guy. It's like having an imaginary friend that you can blame stuff on.

So first John sets the scene: Jesus is descending majestically from the clouds, and everyone on earth gets a good look. Now the vision becomes quantum. Everything is happening in all times, spaces, places, and dimensions. God proclaims, "I am the Alpha and Omega. The one who was, is, and is to come." It doesn't get any more quantum than that.

So John receives a special message for each of the churches in Ephesus, Smyrna, Pergamum, Thyatira, Sardis, Philadelphia, and Laodicea. The theme was pretty much consistent: Jesus is coming, so look busy!

The letter to the church in Laodicea is one of my particular favorites because of its vivid imagery. Presumably God is speaking and says, "I know your works. I know that you are neither hot nor cold. So because you are lukewarm, I will spew you out of my mouth." There's a delightful picture, God puking. The Laodicean church must have felt the same way Adam did: Uh-oh. Dad's mad.

Then Jesus puts in his two cents, "Behold I stand at the door and knock." Does the Savior and Redeemer of the world really need to ring the bell?

AΩ

SCROLLS AND PLAGUES

John must have gambled a bit, and his lucky number seemed to be seven. Now John describes the opening of seven sealed scrolls. Jesus, the Lamb, does the honors. The first four seals he breached set loose the four horseman of the apocalypse. Humanity, created by a loving and intelligent God, has now been tossed in the crapper and flushed. Wars, famines, natural disasters, and diseases are what those in the final days have to look forward to. Although, quite honestly, I can't see how these things can have a novel impact on humankind. It's not like we've never heard of them.

TRUMPETS

After the letters and plagues come the trumpets, because nothing makes you feel better about bad news than a little music.

Seven angels were standing at the ready with their trumpets waiting for the downbeat, and when it comes, the shit really hit the fan.

The first trumpet brought hail, fire, and blood. I wouldn't want to be driving when that happened. The second trumpet cued a flaming mountain to fall into the sea. A third of the sea turned to blood, and a third of the ships in the sea were wrecked. Only God could contain blood and shipwrecks to just a third of the ocean. The third trumpet heralded a flaming star to fall from the sky. This just gets better and better.

By the time the angel blows the seventh trumpet, planet earth is pretty much derelict real estate. Loud voices cried from heaven, "The kingdom of the world now belongs to our Lord." You really have wonder why the Lord would be interested in a planet that was just burned, blitzed, and bled on.

Amy Adams Squire

THE WOMAN AND THE DRAGON

The next of John's enigmatic visions involves a pregnant lady and a big red dragon. The pregnant woman ostensibly represents Israel, from which the Messiah will come. The big red dragon with its seven heads and ten horns is Satan, waiting to devour her child.

I would like to point out at this juncture that time had not been kind to either God or Satan. When they started out in Choose Your Own Adventure: Planet Earth*, both were civil. They negotiated, as in the case of Job. By the time of John's vision of the end of days, they are competing to see who can be the most outrageous. Perhaps it is time to return to the beginning, or even a different beginning, which is, in fact, what happens.

THE BEAST

At last we come to the dreaded beast of apocalyptic lore. This unlovely creature was part goat, part dragon. I suspect it was created in an MIT genetics laboratory after hours by a couple of interns doing vodka shots.

Now this beast wanted everyone for himself, and so what precious little of humanity survived was marked by the beast, possibly an implanted RFID** chip. This mark was necessary to conduct commerce, receive healthcare, obtain housing and education, and so forth. The Bible is quite explicit. The number of the beast was its name, and it was 666. In computer binary code, this translates as 001101100001101100110110. This isn't like a nightclub stamp. This is permanent. With it, you're doomed. Without it, your screwed. You pick. Remember, with God you always have choices. It's just that the choices used to be more attractive.

AΩ

NEW CREATION

The planet looks like it's been through a cosmic blender, and the survivors are enslaved to a digital beast, but things are really looking up. A new Jerusalem drops from the sky. The old heaven and earth are discarded in favor of a bright shiny new heaven and earth. John writes:

I heard a loud voice from the throne saying, "Behold God's dwelling is with the human race. He will dwell with them and they will be his people, and God himself will always be with them as their God. He will wipe every tear from their eyes, and there shall be no more death or mourning, wailing or pain, the old order has passed away.

Behold, I make all things new.

Well, amen to that!

---

*Choose Your Own Adventure is a popular series of children's gamebooks.

**Radio frequency identification.

CPSIA information can be obtained
at www.ICGtesting.com
Printed in the USA
FSOW04n1051181016
26148FS